# I am the Music Man

illustrated by Debra Potter

**Child's Play (International) Ltd**
Swindon          Auburn ME          Sydney
© 2005 Child's Play (International) Ltd     Printed in China
ISBN 1-904550-34-7
1 3 5 7 9 10 8 6 4 2
www.childs-play.com

I am the Music Man,
I come from down your way,
And I can play!
What can you play?
I play piano!

Pi-a, pi-a, pi-a-no,
Pi-a-no, pi-a-no,
Pi-a, pi-a, pi-a-no,
Pi-a, pi-a-no!

I am the Music Man,
I come from down your way,
And I can play!
What can you play?
I play the saxophone!

Saxo, saxo, saxophone,
Saxophone, saxophone,
Saxo, saxo, saxophone,
Saxo, saxophone!

Pi-a, pi-a, pi-a-no etc.

I am the Music Man,
I come from down your way,
And I can play!
What can you play?
I play the bass drum!

Big bass, big bass, big bass drum,
Big bass drum, big bass drum,
Big bass, big bass, big bass drum,
Big bass, big bass drum!

Saxo, saxo, saxophone etc.
Pi-a, pi-a, pi-a-no etc.

I am the Music Man,
I come from down your way,
And I can play!
What can you play?
I play the xylophone!

Xylo, xylo, xylophone,
Xylophone, xylophone,
Xylo, xylo, xylophone,
Xylo, xylophone!

Big bass, big bass, big bass drum etc.
Saxo, saxo, saxophone etc.
Pi-a, pi-a, pi-a-no etc.

I am the Music Man,
I come from down your way,
And I can play!
What can you play?
I play the violin!

Vi-o, vi-o, vi-o-lin,
Vi-o-lin, vi-o-lin,
Vi-o, vi-o, vi-o-lin,
Vi-o, vi-o-lin!

Xylo, xylo, xylophone etc.
Big bass, big bass, big bass drum etc.
Saxo, saxo, saxophone etc.
Pi-a, pi-a, pi-a-no etc.

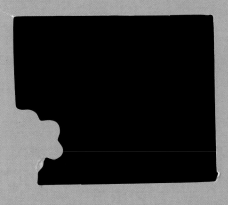

I am the Music Man,
I come from down your way,
And I can play!
What can you play?
I play the trombone!

Trom-bo, Trom-bo, Tro-om-bone,
Tro-om-bone, tro-om-bone,
Trom-bo, Trom-bo, Tro-om-bone,
Trom-bo, tro-om-bone!

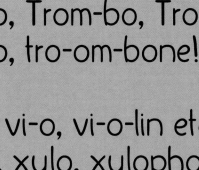

Vi-o, vi-o, vi-o-lin etc.
Xylo, xylo, xylophone etc.
Big bass, big bass, big bass drum etc.
Saxo, saxo, saxophone etc.
Pi-a, pi-a, pi-a-no etc.